W9-ACK-282

DUE

	PRINTED IN U.S.A.

BAND GEEKS
Nothing but Treble

http://www.band217.com

BAND 217

Morgan Bryant
Bandleader

Colby Ellis
Band Founder

Lemuel Soriano
Trumpet

Quentin
Guit

Nantz
board

Calico

An Imprint of Magic Wagon
abdopublishing.com

by Amy Cobb
Illustrated by Anna Cattish

In honor of L.M.E.S. Lakers Beginner Band.
And with sincerest gratitude to Mr. Vaught, who has
instilled a love of music in the hearts of many. —AC

abdopublishing.com

Published by Magic Wagon, a division of ABDO,
PO Box 398166, Minneapolis, Minnesota 55439.
Copyright © 2017 by Abdo Consulting Group, Inc.

Printed in the United States of America, North Mankato, Minnesota.
102016
012017

THIS BOOK CONTAINS
RECYCLED MATERIALS

Written by Amy Cobb
Illustrated by Anna Cattish
Edited by Megan M. Gunderson
Designed by Christina Doffing
Art Directed by Candice Keimig

Publisher's Cataloging-in-Publication Data

Names: Cobb, Amy, author. | Cattish, Anna, illustrator.
Title: Nothing but treble / by Amy Cobb ; illustrated by Anna Cattish.
Description: Minneapolis, MN : Magic Wagon, 2017. | Series: Band geeks
Summary: Colby Ellis starts a garage band with Benton Bluff Junior High
    friends and some fresh faces, but the groups have trouble getting
    along, leading to a schism.
Identifiers: LCCN 2016947369 | ISBN 9781624021749 (lib. bdg.) |
    ISBN 9781624022340 (ebook) | ISBN 9781624022647 (Read-to-me
    ebook)
Subjects: LCSH: Bands (Music)--Juvenile fiction. | Junior high
    schools--Juvenile fiction. | Middle schools--Juvenile fiction.
Classification: DDC [Fic]--dc23
    LC record available at http://lccn.loc.gov/2016947369

TABLE OF CONTENTS

Chapter 1 PITCH PERFECT p. 4

Chapter 2 YOU'RE HIRED p. 14

Chapter 3 AUDITION DAY p. 25

Chapter 4 BAND RULES p. 36

Chapter 5 BOSS OF THE BAND p. 47

Chapter 6 BAND IN A BARN p. 57

Chapter 7 AMATEUR FIGHT p. 67

Chapter 8 CHATTING WITH RUBE p. 79

Chapter 9 PRACTICE TIMES TWO p. 90

Chapter 10 MEET THE GEEKS p. 101

Chapter 1
PITCH PERFECT

"Hey, look out!" I said.

Too late. Morgan Bryant's humongo clipboard, which she always carried around, accidentally bumped into my music stand. That's all it took to send pages of sheet music fluttering to the floor in room 217, the Benton Bluff Junior High band room.

"Oops, sorry!" Morgan said.

"It's okay," I said, shielding my saxophone from her clipboard. That thing was clearly an unlicensed weapon. I was afraid my instrument could be its next victim.

Both of us bent down at the same time to pick up my sheet music, and Morgan nearly gave me a concussion when the bell of her clarinet bonked me on the top of my head.

4

"Ouch!" I said.

"Are you okay?" Morgan asked.

"I probably will be," I said. "If I haven't lost too much blood." I rubbed my head and inspected my fingers, pretending to check for bleeding.

Morgan really looked worried then, so I quickly added, "That was a joke."

"Oh, right." She looked relieved.

Morgan wasn't used to my jokes yet. That's because it was a new school year. Besides learning how to play music together, we were also sort of figuring out who clicked with whom. So far, I wasn't sure if Morgan and I did. Or didn't. But I was about to find out.

See, today's class began with some basics, like reviewing breathing exercises, good posture, and correct embouchure. You know, the usual stuff. Then Mr. Byrd, our band director, threw in something new. He paired us up with other students to practice adjusting our pitch to match that of different instruments. And Morgan was my partner.

"I think this belongs to you," Morgan said, holding up a piece of paper that had been sandwiched between my pages of sheet music.

Of course it was mine. *Colby Ellis* was written on it in my very own handwriting. Right below *Top Secret*.

"Thanks!" I reached for it before Morgan got a good look at everything else written on the page.

She must be one of those super speed-reading kids who can read, like, 1,000 words in one minute. Because before I could snatch it away, Morgan said, "Worn Tread Tirez, Static Brakez, Right Turn Signalz . . . . What are you, a mechanic, or something?" she asked.

"No!" I said, sounding a little more defensive than I meant to.

Morgan didn't seem to notice, though. "I got it," she went on. "You're a race car driver. Right?"

Then she made these kind of annoying racetrack sounds.

"Wrong again," I said. "It's nothing. Seriously." I grabbed for the paper a second time.

But Morgan pulled it away. I felt like Charlie Brown trying to kick the football, only Morgan was my Lucy. She kept pulling it out from under me.

"It must be something important," Morgan said, "since you don't want me to read it."

"Really, it isn't." I held out my hand. "Can I please just have my paper back?"

Morgan finally handed it over. "Sure. But here's a tip. FYI, you don't make words plural by adding a *z* to the end."

"What are you talking about?"

"I'm talking about the way you wrote *tirez*, *brakez*, and *signalz*. It's all misspelled. You're supposed to add an *s* to the end of words to make them plural, not a *z*."

I was about to give Morgan a little FYI of my own—*I don't care!*—but Mr. Byrd came over.

"Colby, Morgan, how's it going?" he asked.

"Good, sir," Morgan said.

I wouldn't exactly say things were "good." So far, Morgan had knocked over my sheet music, read my top secret note, and basically told me I'm a lousy speller. I wanted to switch partners.

But Mr. Byrd went on, "Excellent! So here's what I want you to do. Morgan, you'll play an F concert pitch by yourself. Colby, you will, too. Then you'll both play the same note together."

Mr. Byrd pointed at Morgan. "And go!"

So Morgan played an F note on her clarinet.

Mr. Byrd nodded. "Colby, it's your turn."

I blew into my saxophone's mouthpiece and played my note, too.

"And together!" he said, pumping his fist into the air.

When we were finished, Morgan said, "Your cheeks were too puffy, Colby. Try firming them a little more."

Great. Now Morgan was giving me a hard time about my saxophone skills, too. And to make it even worse, she did it right in front of Mr. Byrd. I didn't want to look bad in front of my band director. Who would?

Anyway, Mr. Byrd apparently thought Morgan was some kind of junior high band genius. He smiled and said, "I'm impressed that you noticed, Morgan! And this is exactly the kind of communication-building exercise that I hoped for.

Keep at it, you two!" Then he moved on to working with two other woodwind players, Sherman Frye and Baylor Meece.

I guess Morgan noticed I wasn't too happy about her calling me out on my technique in front of Mr. Byrd.

"I'm sorry if I embarrassed you. I didn't mean to," Morgan said. "You sounded great. I was just trying to help."

"No problem," I said. "I wasn't embarrassed." Truth! I totally wasn't embarrassed. Really, I was just plain annoyed by Morgan and how she acted like she knew so much.

She smiled. "Good. I hope to be a famous conductor someday at Carnegie Hall in New York."

That reminded me of that "New York, New York" song that Frank Sinatra sang. I started the first few lines with, "Start spreading the news . . ."

Morgan ignored me. Instead, she looked all dreamy and said, "There are hardly any women musical conductors in the whole entire world, you know."

I ended my song and Morgan went on with, "And I want to be the next one to lead an orchestra on the big stage."

"Yeah, well, for now, you'd better jet your brain back from New York City to Benton Bluff. We've gotta work on getting our pitch together," I said right before positioning my mouthpiece and playing another F concert pitch.

"Much better!" Morgan said. "You didn't look like a baby chipmunk that time."

"Thanks. I think."

Morgan and I worked on playing our note together over and over. By the time Mr. Byrd came around to listen to us again, we sounded pretty awesome together.

Mr. Byrd noticed, too. "What an improvement, Morgan and Colby! I'd say you two are almost pitch perfect."

"It's easy when I'm working with someone like Colby." Morgan smiled. "He's a great sax player."

I smiled, too. "You're not so bad either, Miss Music Conductor."

And I actually meant it. At first, Morgan seemed like a real pain. But the more we played together, the more I realized that Morgan wasn't such a bad partner after all. She was just super into music, probably because of how she wanted to be some famous conductor.

Mr. Byrd smiled, too. "Harmony in the band room. That's what I like to hear!"

When Mr. Byrd moved on to the next pair, Morgan said, "Since I'm not so bad, now will you tell me what that top secret note was all about?"

Morgan was back to that, huh? I wasn't sure if I should tell her or not. What if she went and blabbed it to the whole band? But Morgan didn't seem like a blabby blabbermouth.

"Promise you won't laugh?" I said.

Morgan made a cross over her heart.

"And promise not to tell anybody else?"

"I, Morgan Bryant, do solemnly promise that I will not laugh at whatever Colby Ellis is about to tell me, nor will I ever tell anyone else. That is my last will and testament." She pretended to zip her lips. She even locked them up and tossed the key over one shoulder, for good measure.

That made it sound all official. So before I could change my mind, I said, "Those are some names I'm kicking around for my band."

"But," Morgan blinked, "Benton Bluff already has a name."

"No!" I shook my head. "Not this band. I want to start my own band, like on the side."

I waited. Morgan didn't laugh. Or say anything. She finally said, "You know what you need, Colby?"

"What?"

"You need a bandleader." She pointed to herself. "Like me!"

Chapter 2

YOU'RE HIRED

Morgan kept her promise. She didn't tell anybody else my secret. But for the rest of the week, she hung out at my locker and talked nonstop about starting a band.

On Tuesday, Morgan asked, "So, have you picked a name yet?" On Wednesday, she reminded me, "I'd make the most amazing bandleader ever!" And on Thursday, she said, "What good is having a dream if you don't, you know, actually do something about it, Colby?"

Morgan did have a good point. That night, I dreamed I had tons of helium-filled balloons on strings. Then they all started popping. I couldn't stop them. Pop! Pop! Pop! Right before I woke up, all I had was a handful of deflated balloons.

That dream must've been a sign. So on Friday, before Morgan had the chance to say anything, I said, "I decided to go for it. I'm starting my own band!"

"Seriously?" Morgan shrieked.

"Shhh," I shushed her. "Seriously. But I don't want everyone else to know just yet. I still have a lot of stuff to do, you know."

Morgan nodded. "That makes sense. I mean, it's not like—*bam!*—you decide to start a band one day, and it just happens. You have to have a plan first."

"Exactly!" I smiled. Even if I hadn't known Morgan for very long, she totally got where I was going with this.

"And of course, you can't do it all by yourself. You'll definitely need me to be the bandleader, right?"

I leaned against my locker, pretending to think about it.

"Colby!" Morgan nudged me. "I'm perfect for the job. You'd be crazy not to hire me."

"Okay, you're hired!" I gave in.

"Yes!" Morgan jumped up and down.

"Hey, watch it!" I said. "You almost hit me with your clipboard."

Morgan hugged her clipboard tightly. "Sorry," she said. "It's just, this band is going to be awesome. And I'm super excited!"

I smiled. "I can tell."

Morgan didn't waste any time getting started either. "Meet me tomorrow at Five Buys Pizza Pies," she said.

"What time?"

She flipped to a calendar on her clipboard. "How about one o'clock?"

"That works for me," I said.

"Perfect!" Morgan smiled.

When my mom dropped me off at Five Buys Pizza Pies the next day, Morgan was already there.

"Colby!" She waved. Then when I slid into the booth across from her, she said, "We have tons of stuff to do today!"

"Can we at least order lunch first? I'm starved!" I said.

Morgan laughed. "Of course!"

But as soon as the waiter took our order, Morgan started in again. "Check this out." She unclipped some sheets from her clipboard and handed them to me. "You're going to love it, Colby!"

"What is all this?" I asked, skimming over the first page.

"This," Morgan pointed, "is a list of things we have to do to take our band from a dream to a reality."

I frowned because for half a second it bugged me the way Morgan said "our band." I mean, until now, this whole band thing had sort of been in my head. I'd never shared my idea with anybody. But I knew I was being dumb. After all, I couldn't form a band all by myself. So of course, Morgan was right. It really was our band. It might take me a while to get used to the idea, was all.

Morgan must've noticed I wasn't smiling. "Are you okay, Colby?" she asked. "You don't like my ideas, do you?" She reached for the papers she'd handed me.

"No, it's not that," I said. "It's just, starting a band takes a lot of work."

Morgan leaned back against the overstuffed, leather booth cushions. "That's why you're lucky to have me helping you. You won't have to worry about a thing with a bandleader like me on board."

She seemed so sure of herself, and it made me wonder something. "Have you ever started a band before?"

Morgan didn't have a chance to answer. The waiter brought over a couple of glasses of pink lemonade then. "Your pizza will be ready in about fifteen minutes," he said.

"Great! Thanks," I said.

"We better get busy," Morgan said, pulling out a pen. "First thing is choosing a band name."

"I already have a list of names," I said, sipping my lemonade.

Morgan scrunched her nose. "Can I be honest here?"

"Sure." I shrugged.

"Not to hurt your feelings or anything, but those names are sort of stink-o-ville."

Yeah, that didn't exactly hurt my feelings. But I also totally didn't see that one coming. I liked those names. A lot!

"Think about it," Morgan rushed on. "Worn Tread Tirez, Static Brakez, Right Turn Signalz. Those all sound like names straight out of some car magazine, right?"

I nodded.

"For a band name, we should choose a name that appeals to lots of different groups of people. Am I right?"

That did make sense. My favorite bands didn't have names that sounded like they played in a greasy garage, so our band probably shouldn't either. "I guess you're right," I finally said.

"I know I am!" Morgan smiled. "Anyway, we don't have to choose a name right now. But on page two are some of my suggestions." She flipped to the page and pointed.

Possible Band Names

1. Picking Wildflowers
2. Pitching Notes
3. The Bluff's on You

"So what do you think of my ideas?" Morgan asked.

I read them again. "The first one's too girly. And Pitching Notes is too cutesy."

Morgan nodded. "So number three it is!"

"Wait!" I said. "I sort of like that one because of the word play with Benton Bluff being our city. But it's pretty long. How about . . ."

Morgan tapped her pen on the table, waiting for me to come up with something.

"I'll think about it," I finally said when I couldn't come up with anything that sounded better. "We shouldn't rush into choosing just any name. And we've got time."

At first, I didn't think Morgan was going for my idea of waiting. But then she said, "Okay, but don't wait too long. Our name is super important."

"I'll keep brainstorming," I promised. "So what's next?"

"Well," Morgan pointed to the next item on her list, "what kind of band is this? You know, are we forming a jazz band? Bluegrass? Or pop?"

"None of those. I must've forgotten to mention it," I said.

"Mention what?"

"We're forming a punk rock band!" I grabbed a couple of forks and drummed a beat on the table. Then I whipped my head back and forth. "C'mon, Morgan!"

She shook her head. "No way! Please tell me you're joking."

I laughed. "Totally!"

"Good! For a second, I thought I wasn't the best leader for this band, after all." Then she looked all serious. "So for real, what kind of music will we play? You've thought about it, right?"

Wrong. Even though I'd wanted to start my own band for forever, I hadn't really thought about what kind of music I'd like to play. I mean, I loved all kinds of music. That was it! "How about eclectic?" I said. "We can play different genres of music."

"I'm not so sure eclectic is a genre," Morgan said.

"That's perfect," I said. "See, we're already setting a trend."

Morgan smiled. "I'm pretty sure you came up with that idea like two seconds ago, Colby."

I laughed. "Hey, you can't prove it!"

Our waiter came over then and placed a steaming pizza on our table. "One large pepperoni with extra cheese," he said.

"Thanks!" Morgan said.

While we ate, we decided a few more things about our band. Auditions would be at my house next week. Since I had a garage, practices would be at my house, too. And Morgan was in charge of making flyers to advertise the auditions.

Before we left the restaurant, I said, "One more thing. We should probably keep this on the down-low at school."

Morgan looked confused. "Why?"

I shrugged. I had a secret reason why I didn't want any band kids from school joining this band, too. A big reason. But I wouldn't tell anybody else. Not even Morgan. She wouldn't get it.

So on the spot, I came up with, "We already practice with our school band, so maybe we can get some other kids to join our new band. It'll be fun to play with a whole different group. Agreed?"

Morgan didn't look too happy about it, but she nodded. "Agreed."

Chapter 3

AUDITION DAY

"Who's next?" I asked. It was the following weekend already. Morgan and I had spent the whole week handing out flyers to advertise auditions for our new band, making sure we didn't give any to the room 217 band kids. Now finally it was the big day—audition day.

We'd set up some chairs and a sign-in table. We even had score sheets for each person who auditioned. It all looked pretty professional. Or at least as professional as it gets hanging out in a garage with boxes piled all around. If I looked straight ahead, I could almost pretend the assorted holiday decorations, to-be-donated clothes, and last century's odds-and-ends small kitchen appliances didn't even exist out here.

Anyway, Morgan checked her clipboard and said, "Quentin Marret."

"Wait'll you hear him. That guy owns the guitar." I waved him over then. "Yo, Quentin! You're up!"

Quentin looked nervous. "Thanks for inviting me to audition," Quentin said.

"You were the first guitar man I thought of."

Quentin smiled. "So when should I play?"

"Whenever you're ready," Morgan said.

Quentin got right to it. First, he strummed a slow, rhythmic song. I swayed along in my seat.

And when he went right into this rocking riff, I thought Morgan was going to bop right out of her chair. She even clapped when Quentin was finished.

I leaned over and whispered, "I told you that dude was awesome."

"You sure did!" Then she looked Quentin's way and said, "Wow! Who's your guitar instructor?"

"Nobody," Quentin said.

Morgan laughed, like it was the funniest joke ever.

"I'm not kidding," Quentin said.

I could tell Morgan didn't believe him.

"He's totally serious," I said.

Morgan still wasn't buying it. "Tell me how you learned to play then," she said, crossing her arms.

"In the beginning, I watched a lot of video tutorials online," Quentin explained. "After a while, I just picked it up. Now I play mostly by ear. And my sister would probably say I basically never stop."

Morgan didn't look quite as impressed when she said, "By ear, huh?" She jotted something down on Quentin's score sheet, but I couldn't read it. Then she said, "I don't remember seeing you around school before."

"That's because I don't go to your school," Quentin said.

Morgan looked surprised.

Quentin smiled and said, "I live around here, but I'm homeschooled."

"Really?" Morgan said. "I've heard of homeschooling, but I've never actually met anyone who does it."

"Before you ask," Quentin went on, "yes, my mom is my teacher. And no, we don't sit around in our pajamas all day."

Now Morgan smiled. "I wasn't going to ask that, but it's good to know."

"So when will I know if I made the cut, or not?" Quentin asked.

"I think we can make a decision right now," I said.

Morgan held up her hand and said, "Just a sec, Quentin." Then she leaned closer to me and whispered, "What are you doing?"

"I'm giving Quentin the lead guitar gig," I said. "I mean, he is the best guitarist we've heard today."

"Colby, you can't just hire him on the spot."

"Why not?" I asked. Waiting didn't make any sense to me.

"Because we still have to tally scores," Morgan said, still whispering. "Otherwise, the other guitarists could accuse us of not being fair."

I nodded. "Gotcha."

So Morgan turned to Quentin and said, "We'll call you if you got the job."

Quentin came over to shake hands and thanked us again for listening to him play. After he left, I said, "That was a smooth move, Morgan. You know, telling Quentin we'd call him if he got the job. I mean, he's definitely got it."

Morgan shook her head. "I wouldn't be so sure, Colby. His scores might not add up. There was that other guitarist, Derek. He wasn't half bad."

"Are you kidding?" I couldn't believe her. Derek was okay, but Quentin could play guitar circles around him. "What gives?"

"What do you mean?" Morgan asked.

"I mean, why don't you want Quentin in our band? Is it because he's homeschooled?"

Morgan frowned. "Don't be silly, Colby. That has nothing to do with it. Quentin has talent. And besides," she went on, "he's pretty cute."

"That'd be perfect if we were starting a junior high dating club, instead of a band." I rolled my eyes. "If he has talent and you think he's so cute, why don't you think Quentin is right for the band?"

"It's simple. Derek can read sheet music, and Quentin plays by ear. So Derek is a more solid musician. Period."

Morgan had totally lost her mind. I stood up and paced back and forth between a stack of my parents' old yearbooks and a broken fish tank.

"Is this our first disagreement?" Morgan asked, never giving me a chance to answer. "Because if it is, that's a good thing. That means we're learning how to work together."

I just hoped I wasn't learning the hard way that I'd made a mistake in letting Morgan be a part of the band.

"I'm going to be a Carnegie Hall conductor someday," Morgan went on, "so I know what I'm talking about. But since we're tallying scores later, let's just talk about this later, too. Okay?"

She was right. There wasn't any point in arguing right now. Besides, talking about it later gave me more time to convince Morgan that Quentin should be in our band.

"Okay," I said, sliding back into my seat beside Morgan. "Who's next?"

Morgan flipped to a brand new sheet clipped to her board. "Kara Nantz." Then she looked to the row of chairs we'd set up outside of the garage. That's where the kids sat until it was their turn to audition.

Kara came in and played her keyboard for us. After that, Casey Mayes played his trumpet. Then Tyler Jarvis auditioned for lead singer. We were down to one more name on our list, Shanna Snodgrass.

"Shanna, you're up!" I said. But she never came into the garage.

"I guess Shanna's a no-show," Morgan said, crossing her name from our list.

Then we heard a new voice from outside.

"Good! Because I want to audition in her spot, *mademoiselle*!"

I knew without looking up that it had to be Lemuel Soriano. Lem was the only person I knew who spoke French. I hadn't known him long, but I'd already found out when he wasn't playing his trumpet, he was big-time into genealogy. He'd discovered some French royalty ancestor, and he was hoping there were more.

"Wait a minute!" I said. "Nobody from the Benton Bluff band room was supposed to know about this new band. How'd you find out about auditions today, Lem?"

Lem smiled. "*Monsieur*, that's easy. Being a genealogist is like being a detective. Dig around enough," he wiggled his eyebrows up and down, "and you find out all sorts of cool stuff."

"But Lem, you already work so hard in our school band. You're the trumpet section leader and everything. You might not have the time for another band, too," I reasoned.

"Sure I do!" Lem said. "And I'm the best trumpet player you've heard all day."

Plus, Lem was super modest, too. Not! But honestly, he did have me there. Everybody knew Lem was tops at playing his trumpet.

I looked at Morgan. "What do we do now?"

"We let him audition," she said.

I got the feeling Morgan was happy Lem showed up. As upset as she'd been about Quentin playing by ear, I figured it had something to do with the way Lem could read sheet music forward and backward. And probably even in his sleep, too.

So anyway, Lem auditioned. And he was right when he said earlier that he was the best. I mean, there wasn't even a comparison between Lem's trumpet skills and Casey's.

"Lem! You've got to be in our band!" Morgan said when he'd finished playing.

"Not so fast," I jumped in. "We still have to tally audition scores. Remember?" Hey, that's what Morgan had said earlier when I wanted to let Quentin in the band right away. I smiled all sweetly.

"Of course," Morgan said. "We'll give you a call if you got the spot, Lem."

When Lem closed his trumpet case, I thought of something. Maybe Morgan and I could make a deal. I got to pick Quentin to join the band, and she got to pick Lem. It worked out perfectly. As long as Lem was the only other school band member in our new band, that is.

Chapter 4

BAND RULES

Morgan and I spent the next couple of days tallying the audition scores and making final decisions. We called everybody with the top scores. And after school on Thursday, we had our first official band practice in my garage.

As usual, Morgan had her clipboard. She kicked off practice with a roll call. "When I say your name, please raise your hand. I'll begin," she said, raising her hand. "I, Morgan Bryant, will play clarinet. Or conduct. And most important, I am bandleader."

She paused all dramatically. I wasn't sure if she was waiting for everybody to clap or what. But when no one did, Morgan went on with, "Colby Ellis."

I raised my hand.

Morgan said, "You all know Colby is our saxophone player and band founder."

Band founder had a nice ring to it. I couldn't keep from smiling.

"Kara Nantz!" Morgan called next.

She raised her hand and said, "Here!"

"Thank you, Kara," Morgan said. "Everyone, Kara will play the keyboard. Now we have two band members left. Lemuel Soriano."

Lem raised his hand.

"Lem will play trumpet," Morgan said. "And then last we have Quentin Marret playing guitar."

"He's last, but not least," I jumped in.

Morgan shot me a look. "Colby, I wasn't finished."

"Sorry," I said.

"No problem," she said. "Now, as bandleader—"

"Wait!" Kara interrupted. "Is this, like, the entire band? There were way more people than this at the auditions last week."

Morgan nodded. "This is everybody for now. We decided that not everyone who auditioned was the right fit for our band. Right, Colby?"

"Right," I said. "But we're still looking for new band members. Hopefully, there will be even more at our next practice."

"Once people find out how great our band is, everybody will want in," Morgan said confidently. "Now, as your leader, I realize it's important to have certain rules and regulations for all band members to follow. That's why I made everyone a list."

Quentin's eyebrows shot up when he looked at me and said, "Rules. Is she for real?"

I shrugged. Morgan's band rules and regulations were news to me, too. But apparently she was totally for real. She unclipped papers from her board and began handing them out to us.

"Let's run through our band bylaws together," Morgan continued. "Number one, thou shalt not be late for practice. As in ever. Got it?"

When everyone nodded, Morgan went on with rule number two. That one was about not speaking when our bandleader was speaking. Completing a daily practice log was Morgan's third rule. "Don't worry!" she said. "I have copies of practice logs for you, too."

Kara leaned over and whispered, "I wasn't worried."

"Me neither." I grinned.

Honestly, I sort of zoned out after that. This wasn't exactly what I had in mind when I dreamed of starting my own band. I mean, Morgan had more band rules than Mr. Byrd. Having my own band at my house was supposed to be fun. And Morgan was sucking the fun right out of it, one rule at a time.

Then Morgan got to rule eleven, which was our band dress code. She looked over the top of her clipboard at me. "Colby, you especially need to pay attention to this one."

"What's wrong with the way I dress?" I looked down at my T-shirt. *Great Smoky Mountains* was written underneath a snowcapped mountain scene. It was one of my favorite shirts from my family's vacation a few years ago.

"You wear a vacation T-shirt, like, every day," Morgan began. "That one even has a hole in it."

"Where?" I looked all over my shirt.

Morgan pointed. "Right there."

"That's a tiny hole," I said. "This is still a perfectly good shirt."

"But it's not so good for our band's image. Whether we like it or not, people will judge us on our appearance before we ever play one single note," Morgan said. "And maybe you can lose the sunglasses clipped to the neck of your T-shirt, too, Colby."

"But vacation T-shirts and sunglasses are my image," I said. "Everybody looks cooler in sunglasses, you know."

Morgan scrunched her nose. "But you never even wear them. So find another image. Okay?" She went around with suggestions for everyone.

By the time Morgan got to rule seventeen, I wasn't the only one who'd had enough. "Are we going to actually play instruments today, or what?" Quentin asked.

"Be patient," Morgan said. "We'll get to that. But first, I need everyone to sign some forms." She passed around even more sheets. "The first sheet says that you understand our band's bylaws and that you agree to them."

"Man! I forgot to bring a pen," Quentin said.

Morgan reached into a canvas bag with BANDLEADER in lime green puffy paint letters and neon pink band notes scattered all over it. Morgan was super serious about her role in the band.

"Catch!" Morgan said then, tossing everyone pens she pulled from her bag. "I thought of everything."

"*Oui!*" Lem said. "You sure did, *mademoiselle.*"

Lem had been pretty quiet until now. It sort of made me wonder what he thought about Morgan's leadership. Lem looked pretty happy, though, so I figured it didn't bother him.

"The next sheet says you agree not to hold Colby and me responsible for any accidents," Morgan went on.

Quentin stood up. "Basically, that means if I trip over one of these boxes, I promise not to sue you. Right?" He did this exaggerated fake fall and landed on a box of my dad's old comic books. "Help! Help!" he called out, laughing.

"I'll save you!" I said, jumping in to pull him up off the boxes. I tugged on his arm, and Quentin pretended to be stuck.

Everyone laughed. Okay, not everyone. Morgan frowned about us goofing around.

"Will you help me up?" Quentin said, crawling toward Morgan.

"No, you're acting silly." She folded her arms across her chest.

Now Quentin sort of looked offended for real. "We're just having some fun."

"As your bandleader, I take practice very seriously," Morgan began. But then she stopped and got this funny look on her face. It wasn't because of me and Quentin joking around either.

As soon as I turned around, I knew what the problem was. Davis Beadle, Sherman Frye, and Hope James had just showed up. And that was no joke!

"Hey, what's up?" I said, acting all cool.

Hope smiled. "We heard about your band, and we want to join."

"Yeah, it sounds like fun," Davis said.

"We even brought our instruments," Sherman said, holding up his flute.

I flashed Morgan a how-do-we-get-outta-this look. But since I couldn't exactly read Morgan's mind to get an answer, she and I had to chat. Now! "Morgan, can I talk to you for a sec?" I said.

"Sure," she said.

When we were out of earshot, I said, "You promised you wouldn't tell the band kids at school about our new band."

"I didn't," she said.

I guess she could tell I didn't buy it.

"I kept my promise," she went on. "I didn't tell them. Not even one."

"Then who did?" I asked.

It must've hit us at the same time because we both said, "Lem!"

"You didn't tell Lem not to say anything?" I asked.

"No, I thought you did," Morgan said.

"Well, I thought you did. You are the bandleader, after all," I said.

"That's how it always goes," Morgan said. "The bandleader gets blamed for everything." Then she just threw her arms in the air.

She hadn't been bandleader that long, so that was a little dramatic. Neither of us said anything for a minute. Then I got an idea. "That's it! Since you're the bandleader, you should get rid of 'em."

"Me?" Morgan squeaked. "No way, Colby! Besides, we're new to Benton Bluff's school band. If you tell Davis, Sherman, and Hope that they can't be in this band, then we're going to be on the outs in room 217. Is that what you want?"

Morgan was right. That wasn't how I wanted to start off my first year in junior high band. So I knew what I had to do—deal with it.

"Fine!" I said. "But no more room 217 Band Geeks. Okay?"

"Got it!" Morgan smiled. "But you really shouldn't call them the Band Geeks. That sounds sort of mean."

"I don't mean anything by it," I said. "Everybody who loves music is technically a Band Geek. Even me! So really, it's like an honor to be a Band Geek."

"Gotcha!" Morgan said. "We're all Band Geeks."

"Exactly!" I said. I just hoped letting the Benton Bluff Band Geeks into our new band wasn't a mistake. And I hoped I could still keep my secret safe from them.

Chapter 5
BOSS OF THE BAND

For the rest of that first practice, Morgan went over more boring rules. Now it was Saturday, and everyone showed up at my garage for our second practice. And guess who else showed up? Even more Band Geeks from room 217. This was not good!

"Morgan," I grumbled, "this isn't what I had in mind for my own band. This is practically a small orchestra."

She smiled. "I know! Isn't it perfect, Colby?"

Perfect was the last word I'd use to describe what was happening here. I mean, my garage was big enough to fit two cars. But with all of the clutter, I wasn't sure how many more band members we could stuff in here. Plus, besides Quentin and

Kara, everyone else was in Mr. Byrd's band. It was exactly what I didn't want to happen.

But that was probably exactly what Morgan wanted. That way she could practice on us before she made it big-time at Carnegie Hall someday. We were like guinea pigs, except with musical instruments. I pictured Morgan as a furry guinea pig, holding a clipboard, and it made me laugh.

"What's so funny?" Morgan asked.

"It's nothing," I said. "Seriously."

Yulia Glatt jumped in then with, "I heard you need a lead singer."

"We do!" Morgan nodded. "Are you up for it, Yulia?"

"Definitely!" Yulia grinned.

So apparently Yulia didn't even have to audition. That didn't seem fair.

Morgan must've noticed I wasn't too happy about it because she added, "If it's all right with Colby, too, that is."

"Sure," I said, as if I had a choice now that Morgan already told Yulia she could be our lead singer. If I said no, I'd look like a world-class jerk.

"And I can write band bios," Baylor Meece said. "If you need references, I'm a reporter for our school newspaper, the *Bloodhound*."

Everybody knew Baylor was the paper's star reporter. Having Baylor on board wasn't such a bad idea, even if she was in Mr. Byrd's band. We could use the positive press. "You're in!" I said. Hey, if Morgan could make decisions, so could I.

Then Miles Darr wheeled over and said, "And you'll need an online presence, too."

"Online presence?" I hadn't thought about that.

"That's how bands get discovered these days," Miles said. He hooked his thumbs in his suspenders and gave them a little pop, adding, "And you're looking at the best PR man in the biz."

"When you put it like that," I said, "how can I say no?"

"You can't!" Miles held up his hand for a high five.

"Dude!" Kara said when she headed into the garage. "This place is packed."

Morgan smiled. "I told you everybody would want in once they found out our band is awesome."

"I'm not so sure we're awesome," Quentin said. "We haven't even played together yet."

"But we're about to," I said. "What are we waiting for? Let's grab our instruments."

"Yes!" Kara said.

"Hang on!" Morgan waved her clipboard in the air. "Roll call first." And as soon as she finished roll call, Morgan passed out some papers to everyone.

"Hey, what's this?" Quentin asked.

"That," Morgan said, "is called sheet music."

"But I play by ear. I can't read sheet music," Kara said.

"Me neither," Quentin said. "It looks like some foreign language to me." Then he started talking in this made-up language that nobody else could understand, not even Quentin himself.

"Don't worry. I can teach you," Morgan said. She reached for her BANDLEADER bag, whipped out a dry-erase board, and drew some lines. "This is called a staff. See, it has five lines and four spaces."

"Hey, I just noticed something!" Davis said. "You're not in our school band. What school do you go to?"

"I'm homeschooled," Quentin said, his cheeks turning pink. I could tell the extra attention embarrassed him.

"Oh," was all Davis said. Then he glanced at Kara. "You go to our school, but you're not in our band either."

"Dude, forget school band," Kara said. "Right now, all that matters is that we're in this band, the whatever-we're-going-to-call-ourselves band."

"Yeah," Baylor said. "What is this band's name? I need to know for the write-up."

Miles nodded. "And I need to know for the website."

"We're still working on a name," I said. "So stay tuned."

Then it was like a lightbulb went off in my head. "Guys, that could be our first hit song. If you wanna hear the best new band, stay tuned. The best band in all of the land, stay tuned."

Quentin bobbed his head to the beat and even strummed a few chords on his guitar. "I'm digging it. Stay tuned!"

"Stop!" Morgan said. "Before we work on a song, it's really important that Quentin and Kara learn how to read sheet music."

Davis leaned against a box. "That means take a break, everybody. This could take a while."

Yulia shot Davis a look, and he dropped it.

Morgan drew a treble clef on the board then. She drew some notes and told Quentin and Kara the names of the notes, too. "Got it so far?"

"Yeah," Quentin said. "But why do I have to learn that stuff? I mean, just let me play." He started strumming another song on his guitar.

When he was finished, Lem said, "Wow, *monsieur*! You sound like you've been taking lessons all of your life."

Quentin smiled. "Nope. But I have been playing practically all of my life. I got my first guitar when I was four years old."

"You mean, you've been playing guitar for, like, *nine years*?" Davis asked.

"You got it," Quentin said. "How long have you been playing drums?"

"This is my second year in band," Davis said.

Everyone laughed when Quentin said, "Two years, huh? I guess that's a start."

Now Davis's face turned red, and he didn't have much to say after that. Really, nobody had much of a chance to say anything because Morgan assigned everyone their places in the garage.

"From now on, this is your spot for every practice," she said. After that, we played the song she'd brought for us. It was called "Green Cupcakes."

After we'd played it through a few times, Morgan said, "That wasn't too bad."

"*Oui!*" Lem said. "It just wasn't too good either."

"It's only our second practice, though, and our first time playing together outside of room 217. We'll get way better," Morgan promised.

By then, Hope's dad was there to pick her up. Some other parents were showing up, too, so practice was over. Everybody was gone, except Kara and Quentin.

"Dude, can we talk to you?" Kara started in.

"Sure," I said. "What's up?"

Quentin frowned. "Not this band, I'll tell you that."

"Yeah," Kara said. "This isn't exactly the kind of band I thought I was signing up for. I didn't know

Morgan was going to be the boss of the band world."

"I'm with her," Quentin agreed, pointing toward Kara. "When you first told me about starting a band, you said it was going to be fun. *Errrrr!* You were wrong."

"Totally wrong," Kara added.

"Sheet music and assigned seats isn't fun," Quentin continued.

Kara sighed. "I'm sorry, but I don't think I want to be in your band anymore."

"Me neither," Quentin said.

I didn't really blame Kara or Quentin. They were right. This band was supposed to be fun, and it wasn't. I already had Mr. Byrd's band class every day in room 217 with Morgan, Davis, and the others. That was where I learned all about proper technique and playing sheet music. This band was supposed to be about just enjoying the music. At least, I hoped it would be.

"See ya later, Colby," Quentin said.

"See ya," Kara said as they turned to go.

"Wait!" I called after them. "I've got an idea. Just wait."

It would be risky, but I was pretty sure I could make it work.

Chapter 6

BAND IN A BARN

A few days later, I finally put my plan into action. Since Quentin was homeschooled, that meant nobody else from room 217 knew him. So it made perfect sense for Kara and me to secretly meet at his house. Quentin lived on a farm, which felt like the middle of nowhere. My mom dropped us off, and Kara's mom was picking us up.

"I can't believe we're really doing this," Kara said when Quentin met us in front of his house that afternoon.

Quentin looked at me. "Do you still think this is a good idea, Colby?"

"Yep." I nodded. "I don't see any other way."

Quentin picked up his guitar case and said, "Then follow me."

So I grabbed my saxophone case, and Kara held on to the small keyboard she'd brought along. We followed Quentin to a weathered, graying barn and then climbed the ladder leading up to the barn loft. Trust me, getting our instruments to the top wasn't easy, either. But we finally did it.

"Sweet!" Kara said, looking around. "You have a swing up here and everything."

"I told you this was the perfect place for a secret practice," I said. The swing hanging from the rafters and the stack of hay bales gave us plenty of seating. And besides the cows and chickens in the stalls below, nobody else would ever know we were here. Morgan and the other Band Geeks would never find out about our secret practice.

"I can't believe it," Kara said, plopping onto a hay bale. "Morgan's not here with her ginormous clipboard taking roll call and bossing us around."

"Yeah, this is how being in your own band is supposed to be," Quentin agreed.

I definitely agreed, too. For the first time, it felt like my band was going in the direction I wanted it to go in. It wasn't just Morgan making up a bunch of dumb rules for us to follow. "So what do you want to do first?" I asked.

"I brought my notebook," Kara said. "Maybe we can start off by writing some of our own songs."

"Sounds good," I said. I was always coming up with songs off the top of my head.

That was one of the reasons I wanted to start my own band in the first place, to write songs and to play them, too. So hanging out with some other people who were also into songwriting was awesome.

Quentin opened his guitar case and said, "I've had this tune stuck in my brain for a few days." Then he threw his strap around his neck and strummed a few chords.

"That sounds really cool," I said, swaying to the beat.

"I like it, too," Kara agreed. "Do you have any lyrics?"

Quentin shook his head. "Not yet. See, my thing is coming up with different tunes first."

"Gotcha," Kara said. "I'm the total opposite. For me, it's all about getting the lyrics down. The tune comes later. What about you, Colby?"

They both looked at me, like I was supposed to decide who was right. Or wrong. But I wasn't sure, so I said, "Maybe either way works."

That didn't help, though. Quentin insisted the music came before the words. And Kara was positive the story of the song had to be in place before even one note could be played.

"Otherwise," she said, "you'd never be able to match the tone of the music to the words. The whole song would be out of balance."

"You've got it all backward, Kara," Quentin argued. "For me, the tune sets the mood for the words."

"Guys, this reminds me of that whole chicken and egg thing," I said. "Except this is, 'What came first, the melody or the lyrics?'" I pretended to beat my air drum. "Buh-dum-chh."

I laughed, but when Quentin and Kara didn't, I said, "Hey, that was a joke."

Nobody laughed. Again.

"Moving on . . ." I said. "Why don't we brainstorm some ideas for songs we'd like to write about?" That made total sense to me. Plus, we could all agree on some ideas, right?

Wrong!

Because when Kara said we had to write at least one love song, Quentin disagreed. "Love songs are way overdone."

"But it's important to find a topic that everyone can identify with," Kara said. "And that topic is love."

Quentin shook his head. "There are too many love songs out there now. Besides, we're in junior high. What do we know about love? We've got to write a song about something we know. It's gotta come from the gut."

Kara scrunched up her nose. "No way! I'm not writing any songs about guts."

"No, not gut songs. The song has got to come from the gut, though, to make it more real to the audience." Quentin looked at me like he was saying, "Can you believe Kara?"

I was starting to feel sort of uncomfortable again, almost like I was caught in the middle. I halfway wished Morgan was here. If this is what being the bandleader was like, then no thank you! I didn't want the job.

"Maybe we should forget songwriting for now," I said. "Let's just play a few songs together. What's something you guys know?"

Kara gave us a list of love songs she could play. Quentin told us about all of the cool cowboy ballads he knew, like "Git Along Little Doggies."

"Are you kidding?" Kara asked.

Quentin shrugged. "What's wrong with cowboy songs?"

"Hello!" Kara waved her hand in Quentin's face. "You just said we need to play songs about stuff we know. I don't know about Colby, but I know zero about being a cowboy."

"I got it!" I said before they got even further off track. "How about a nice patriotic song?" I licked my lips and began playing the intro of "The Star Spangled Banner" on my sax. The eighth graders at school played it every day, and I'd already learned it just by playing by ear.

I was relieved when Kara and Quentin jumped in to play along with me. Finally, we agreed on something.

Our broad stripes and bright stars had just made it through the perilous fight, and the ramparts we watched were so gallantly streaming, when something totally unexpected happened.

All of the sudden, Quentin's younger sister, Lexie, jumped up from behind a hay bale and belted out the next line. "And the rocket's red glare, the bomb bursting in air!" She didn't stop until we finished the last line about the land of the free and the home of the brave.

When we finished that last note, nobody said anything for a second. It was like the whole barn loft went silent, including the crazy rooster that had been crowing all afternoon.

Then Quentin said, "Lexie, I told you not to bug us. Get out of here!" He pointed toward the ladder that led back down into the barn.

"Hang on!" I said. "I didn't know your sister could sing like that."

"Me neither," Kara said.

Quentin rolled his eyes. "She never stops singing. My life is like one giant music video, starring Lexie."

"That's perfect!" I said.

"It is?" Quentin looked confused.

"Of course! When it's just the three of us practicing, we'll need a lead singer since Yulia isn't around," I went on. "Maybe Lexie could do it. She can be our fill-in."

"I'd love to!" Lexie said. Then she stuck her tongue out at Quentin. "Ha. See? *They* want me around."

Kara laughed and stuck out her tongue, too. "Yeah, Quentin!"

When Quentin laughed, I did, too. It felt really good to be part of a band where everybody got along, at least for right now. And while we were, it was the perfect time to play another song.

"See if you know this one," I said, starting off the first few notes of "America the Beautiful."

When we finished, Quentin said, "Man, we've never sounded better!"

"Agreed!" Kara said, giving everyone a fist bump. Then she went all serious. "So what are we going to do about practicing with the rest of the school band?"

I shrugged. "It's easy. We'll just show up for practice once a week at my garage with Morgan and all of the other Band Geeks from room 217. And then we'll secretly practice once a week here, too. The four of us will be a barn loft quartet." I put my hand in. "Agreed?"

Kara, Quentin, and Lexie put their hands on top of mine. Then everyone said, "Agreed!" all at the same time.

Now we just had to hope no one found out.

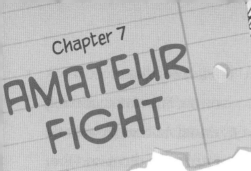

Chapter 7
AMATEUR FIGHT

For the next couple of weeks, my plan totally worked. I'd gone from dreaming about having my own band to being a member of two different bands. Keeping the secret about Quentin, Kara, Lexie, and me practicing on our own was no sweat. At least, it wasn't until Morgan showed up early before practice at my garage one day.

"Colby! I have the biggest news ever!" Morgan said, jumping up and down.

"Don't tell me!" I rubbed my forehead, pretending to be psychic. "We just got a record deal, and our song hit number one on the charts?"

Morgan rolled her eyes. "Puh-lease! Like that would ever happen with Quentin and Kara still learning to read music."

I ignored that one. Morgan and the other room 217 Band Geeks still weren't crazy about having Kara and Quentin in this band. And they were still really hung up on teaching them how to read sheet music and how to play with the proper technique. There'd been a few clashes at practice, but so far, nothing major.

"Anyway," Morgan went on, "this is still huge. Are you ready for it?"

I nodded. "I'm listening."

"I stopped by Jazz Front yesterday, and guess what."

"What?" I asked.

Morgan pulled a flyer from her clipboard. "I picked this up."

"What are you waiting for?" I read. "Bring your sound to Jazz Front's First Annual Amateur Musician Night next Friday night at seven o'clock."

"Isn't it awesome?" Morgan squealed. "This is our first real gig, Colby!"

Rube Chenault was the locally famous owner of Jazz Front. At his shop in town, people could buy anything from old jazz records to song books to new instruments. If Rube was having a night for amateur musicians to come in to play for a crowd, no wonder Morgan was excited.

"How do we sign up?" I asked.

Morgan smiled. "Don't worry. I already took care of everything."

"Wait," I said. "Shouldn't you have talked to the entire band first?"

"Of course not, silly!" Morgan waved her hand. "Who wouldn't jump at this chance?"

"What chance?" Baylor asked, coming up behind us. Some other band members had showed up, too.

"We got our first—" I began.

Before I could finish, Morgan shushed me. "Colby! I'm going to tell everyone at our meeting before practice begins."

"Sorry," I said. "I didn't know we were having a meeting."

"That's why I'm the bandleader," Morgan reminded me.

Actually, she reminded me of that a lot. And how lucky all of us were to have her leading this band. But the way Morgan planned meetings and stuff without telling me didn't make me feel so lucky. Instead, it made me feel really dumb since I wasn't in the loop about stuff that went on in my own band.

That was another thing I liked about having a secret band on the side with Quentin, Kara, and Lexie. It was small enough that everyone had a say in it, not just one person, like with Morgan.

"Baylor," Morgan went on, "I promise I'll let you in on the big news as soon as everyone gets here."

"It sounds exciting!" Baylor got her notepad and pen ready for the scoop.

A few minutes later, the whole band was there.

Well, almost.

"Sorry we're late!" Quentin said. He and Kara got there about five minutes after everyone else.

Morgan leaned over and whispered, "They're always the last ones to show. They better not make us last at Jazz Front's Amateur Night."

"They're not always last," I whispered back. "Try cutting them some slack."

"I already did. Otherwise, they wouldn't even be in this band," Morgan shot back.

I just shook my head.

Morgan took roll call and called the meeting to order then. "Now that everyone is finally here," she said, "I have something super exciting to tell you all."

"What is it?" Sherman jumped in.

"*Oui!*" Lem said. "Tell us, *mademoiselle*."

Morgan held up one hand. "Patience, please. I promise this news is worth waiting for." She held up the flyer she'd shown me earlier and continued.

"I picked up this flyer at Jazz Front. Next Friday at seven o'clock, there's an amateur musician night. Isn't that awesome?"

"What does that mean exactly?" Hope asked.

"It means that our band will go to Rube's shop to perform for an audience," Morgan said. "This is our first gig!"

"We're going to be rich!" Davis said.

"Slow down, Davis. This isn't actually a paying gig," Morgan said.

Davis looked bummed.

"But lots of people will be there to hear us, so you never know," Morgan said. "Maybe someone will hear our band and pay us to play someday."

"We've got to start somewhere," I said.

Morgan nodded. "Exactly!"

The band was so excited, everyone started talking at once.

Morgan clapped her hands to get our attention again. "I have something else to tell you," she said.

"I've already signed us up, but when I registered, I had to write down our band's name."

"But we still don't have a name," Quentin pointed out.

"Make that we *didn't* have a band name," Morgan said. "Since I had to come up with something on the spot, I called us Band 217. Isn't that cool?"

"I get it!" Sherman said. "Room 217 is where we practice at school."

Morgan smiled. "You got it!"

"I love it!" Baylor said, jotting it down in her notebook.

"Hang on," Kara said then. "I don't love it."

Quentin was on Kara's side. "Me neither. Everybody in this band isn't in the school band, you know."

"That is true, *mademoiselle*," Lem said, sort of taking up for them.

"Most of us are, though," Morgan said. "So the majority rules."

"Let's ask our band founder," Quentin said. "What do you think about the name, Colby?"

Talk about being put on the spot! "Maybe you could've asked us first," I began.

"Registration ends today, though," Morgan said. "I had to put something. Would you rather us be called The No-Name Band?"

"She does have a point," I began.

"Perfect! That settles it." Morgan smiled. "Now, let's choose a song to play. I have some ideas."

Quentin muttered under his breath, "She always does."

"What'd you say?" Morgan asked.

"Nothing," he said.

"Just get over it because with Amateur Night being only a week away, we don't have tons of time to prepare," Morgan said.

Then she told us some songs she was thinking of. There was "The Six-Toed Cat," "Seven Ate Nine," and "Red River Blues."

"Okay, let's put it to a vote," Morgan said.

Quentin formed an *X* with his arms. "Errrr!" he said. "I vote none of them."

"You're going to have to choose one," Morgan huffed, "because these are all easier songs for those who can't read sheet music. Wait, that's just you and Kara."

Uh-oh.

I got a bad feeling, like we were headed straight for disaster.

"You know what I think about sheet music?" Quentin asked. Then he grabbed some copies Morgan had brought. "This!" He ripped them into tiny pieces and tossed them up in the air. They rained down like confetti. No kidding! It was super dramatic.

It was like watching those cycling races in the Olympics. When someone wipes out, everyone at the same time goes, "Ohhhhh!" Yeah, that's the sound the whole band made in my garage.

Morgan looked like a volcano about to explode. "This isn't the band for that kind of stuff," she said.

"And this isn't the right band for me. I quit!" Quentin looked at me then. "Sorry, dude." And just like that, he grabbed his guitar and headed home.

"It probably isn't the right band for me either," Kara said. Then she came over and whispered for my ears only, "Colby, if you want our little band to perform at Jazz Front's Amateur Night, too, then sign us up."

When Kara took off right behind Quentin, Morgan's mouth dropped open. I could tell she didn't know what to say.

For like half a second, I thought about storming out of the garage and taking off after Quentin and Kara. But that would be sort of weird because, you know, it was my garage we were hanging out in.

Still, I didn't want to be all alone with the other school band kids. I mean, what if they found out about my big secret? Not the one about the secret band I was in either. Quentin and Kara couldn't leave me alone with them!

"Maybe if you apologize, I can talk them into coming back, Morgan," I finally said.

"No way! We don't need them," Morgan said.

"I think we do, *mademoiselle*," Lem said. Right now, he was the only room 217 Band Geek who seemed to think so.

But Morgan ignored him. "We'll do better at Amateur Night without them." Then she frowned. "So what did Kara whisper to you right before she left, Colby?"

Baylor nodded. "I wondered the same thing."

"Nothing big," I said. Truth! That's because our secret band wasn't big. With only Kara, Quentin, Lexie, and me, it was superduper small.

Chapter 8

CHATTING WITH RUBE

After everyone left my garage that afternoon, I hung out there by myself for a while just thinking about stuff. Mostly it was small stuff. Like how shadows on this one box sort of looked like a giant ketchup bottle I'd seen once when my family made a road trip through Illinois.

But the longer I sat there, the more some big stuff popped into my brain, too. Like what a disaster having my own band was. I wasn't even sure how things became so complicated.

"Hey, Colby!" my mom said then. "I'm running some errands. Want to come?"

At first, I didn't want to. But running errands beat sitting in the garage alone, gazing at imaginary condiment bottles on cardboard.

"Sure," I finally said, hopping in the car and buckling up.

When we pulled onto the road, Mom said, "How was band practice, kiddo?"

"Not so good," I mumbled.

"Oh? I'm sorry to hear that," she said. "You want to talk about it?"

I shook my head. Talking about it wouldn't do any good. It's not like it would make Morgan less bossy. Or make the kids from the school band get over being hung up on playing sheet music and practicing proper technique 24/7. And it wouldn't bring Quentin and Kara back to the band either.

"Okay," Mom said. "But if you change your mind, I'm a good listener. Although, I don't know the first thing about band." She laughed a little.

"That's okay, Mom," I said. "Sometimes I don't think I know much about it myself."

"Colby, that's not true," Mom said, stopping at a red light. "I can tell you've already learned a lot just since this school year started. Do you know what your real problem is?"

"No, what?"

She eased forward on the gas. "You're too hard on yourself, son. Cut yourself some slack."

She made it sound pretty easy. But like she just said, she didn't know the first thing about band. And she definitely didn't know anything about being in a band with kids like Morgan and Lem and Baylor. Those kids were practically junior high band prodigies or something. At least, I thought prodigy meant the same thing as genius.

Anyway, I got a great idea when Mom pulled into Margie's Thimble, a fabric shop where she bought all of her thread and dress patterns. That was something she knew tons about since she worked as a seamstress. But I didn't need any button-sewing tutorials. It was band I needed help with. And who better to talk to than Rube Chenault?

"Mom, can I run over to Jazz Front while you shop?"

"Of course," Mom said. "Just look both ways before you cross the street."

"Mom!" I said. "I am in seventh grade, you know."

Mom smiled. "I know, but that doesn't stop me from fussing over you. I'll come pick you up as soon as I'm finished shopping."

"Got it," I said.

The bells above Jazz Front's door jingled as I headed inside.

Rube looked up from the counter, and he smiled when he saw me. "Colby, my man! How goes it?"

"Not so bad," I said.

"Really? You look sort of down." He came out from behind the counter. "It's not that new saxophone, is it?"

I shook my head.

See, this was where Mom and Dad bought my saxophone when I first signed up for the school band. And Rube had spent tons of time with us that day because he said he liked getting to know all of his customers. Dad had joked on the way home that Rube spent more time talking to us about my sax than the auto salesman had spent selling us our car.

"You sure? It's still under warranty," Rube said.

"Nope, my sax is great," I said.

Rube's eyes got all crinkly when he smiled and said, "Good. I'm glad you stopped in tonight, Colby."

"You are?"

"I sure am," Rube said. "Have you ever felt like you just needed somebody to talk to? Somebody who would really listen to you?"

I nodded.

"That's how I've been feeling all day. Do you have time to sit and chat with this old man?"

"Sure," I said. "My mom's shopping, so we probably have tons of time."

"Let's sit over here," Rube said, "so I can rest my aching feet a while."

I followed Rube over to a table beside a sheet music display.

"Ugh!" I said, sliding into a chair facing away from the glossy music books. I was sick of sheet music. It reminded me of the school band. And Band 217.

Rube pulled out a chair across from me. "Now tell me what those music books have ever done to you," he said.

"Nothing, I guess."

"All right." Rube nodded. "For a second, I thought they were giving you a hard time."

"Nope," I said. "They're just dumb books."

"Dumb books, huh?" Rube laughed then and slapped his knee. "Whoo-wee! Did I ever tell you about the time I started my own band?"

I shook my head.

"Well, I'll tell you now," he began. "My band was going to be the biggest band to ever hit since sound was invented."

"And it was, right?"

Rube shook his head. "Wrong! It lasted all of one day."

"One day?" I said. "But you have albums and everything." Mom even bought one when we stopped in to buy some extra reeds a few weeks ago.

"I sure do," Rube said. "But my first band never made an album. We never even played a whole song together." He lowered his voice, almost to a whisper. "Do you want to know why, Colby?"

I leaned in closer, so I wouldn't miss a word. "Why?"

"Simple. Nobody cared about making music," he said.

"They didn't?"

"No, sir," Rube continued. "Instead, everybody was more interested in being in charge. They were like, 'It's my way, or no way!'"

I was sort of surprised at first. I mean, that sounded a lot like what had happened in Band 217. Morgan and the other kids from school band wanted things to go their way. They wouldn't listen to anybody else.

But then I thought of something. Weren't Kara and Quentin sort of being that way, too? And honestly, so was I. Except, we wanted to have fun and be creative. Instead of playing music, we spent most of our time trying to get the other band kids to do things our way.

"So what did you do?" I asked.

"What could we do?" Rube shrugged. "We broke up."

"That's sort of what happened in my band, too," I said.

Rube looked surprised. "You're kidding!"

"No," I said. And then I told Rube all about how I'd wanted to start my own band. And how Morgan found out about it and pushed her way in. Then more kids from school pushed their way in, too. So Kara, Quentin, and I formed our own secret band with Lexie. I even told him about what happened today and that Kara and Quentin had quit Band 217.

"Whoo-wee! Let me make sure I've got this straight," Rube said. "Now besides your school band, you're in two other bands."

"Exactly," I said.

"But Band 217 doesn't know about the secret band, right?"

I nodded. "You've got it."

Rube leaned back in his chair. "What are you going to do, Colby?" Rube finally asked.

"I'm not sure," I said. "Maybe I want to stay in both bands. Or maybe I don't want to be in either one of them."

"But you have to stay in Band 217. At least, until next Friday night. Morgan told me you'd founded the band when she registered for Amateur Night."

"Amateur Night! Man, I almost forgot about that," I said. "And that reminds me, Kara told me I should sign our secret band up for it, too."

"If you do, it won't be so secret anymore," Rube said.

True.

"But," Rube went on, "it might help you choose the right band for you."

That was true, too. And I liked that idea a lot. As soon as Amateur Night was over, I'd pick the right band for me.

"Rube," I said, "is there still time to register?"

"There sure is, until the store closes tonight." He stood up and said, "But first, always remember this, Colby. Band isn't about the skills. It's all about the people." He smiled. "I'll get your form."

I had just enough time to fill it out before Mom showed up to head home.

"Bye, Rube!" I called on my way out the door.

"I'll see you next Friday," Rube said.

Yeah, at Amateur Night. It was just over a week away, and I had tons to do to get ready for it.

Chapter 9
PRACTICE TIMES TWO

I started by holding a special practice in Quentin's barn loft with him, Kara, and Lexie a couple of days later.

"We're all registered for Amateur Night at Rube's," I said, holding up a copy of the registration form. "Here are the rules."

Lexie snatched it and read, "Each performer is limited to one song only. Performances must be five minutes or less. First, second, and third place trophies will be awarded." She read some more rules about all decisions being final and stuff. And when she got to the end, she said, "Our band's name is Four Ever?"

"Yeah, because there are four of us," I said.

Quentin laughed. "That sounds sort of cheesy."

"But I had to come up with something," I explained.

Then Quentin goofed around saying our band's name in funny ways, like "Four Ev-uh" and "Fourrrr Everrrr."

Kara laughed, too.

Great. Now I got exactly how Morgan felt when they gave her a hard time about the name Band 217. She'd had to choose fast, too.

"It's not *that* funny," I finally said. "Besides, could you come up with anything better?"

Quentin thought about it. "Maybe something like Outer Planet or Astronomy Alliance."

"Are we a band, or some old scientists?" I said.

"Everybody knows space stuff is cool," Quentin said. "Those names are way cooler than Four Ever."

I guess Quentin could tell I was sort of annoyed because he apologized and said, "I'm just joking, dude. Calm down. You're starting to remind me of Morgan."

"Yeah, be careful, Colby," Kara chimed in. "The next thing you know, you'll show up for practice with a clipboard to take roll call."

"Hey, at least she managed to get things done without spending half of practice goofing around."

Quentin looked at Kara. "Are you thinking what I'm thinking?"

Kara nodded and drew an air heart.

"Don't forget their initials," Quentin said, adding them to the invisible heart. "C + M."

"Whatever." I shook my head. "Let's just play. Okay?"

"What should we play?" Lexie asked. "We've mainly been practicing patriotic songs."

"We could do 'Yankee Doodle Dandy,'" Kara said, whistling the chorus.

"Nah," Quentin said. "I mean, it's fun to play and all. But doesn't that one seem too . . . little kiddish?"

I nodded. "That's kind of what I thought, too."

"Or we could play 'The Star Spangled Banner,'" Lexie suggested. "That song is a perfect match for my voice." She sang a few lines to prove it.

Lexie sounded awesome, as usual. But there was one problem. "I almost think that song might be too big for us," I said.

"What do you mean?" Kara asked.

"Think about it," I said. "Our national anthem is played at major events, like the Super Bowl and stuff. But there's only four of us, so maybe our sound wouldn't be big enough to pull it off." I looked around. "I mean, we don't even have a drummer."

Quentin agreed. "Yeah, it probably would sound better if we had a bigger band."

Everybody was quiet for a minute, and I wondered if they were thinking the same thing I was—Band 217 could pull it off. It was almost too bad we weren't all still together. Then Lexie sang the first few lines of "My Country, 'Tis of Thee."

"That's really nice, Lex." I bobbed my head along as she sang. "I vote for that one."

"Me too," Kara agreed.

And so did Quentin.

"'My Country, 'Tis of Thee' wins," I said.

So Kara got her keyboard, Quentin slid his guitar strap over his head, and I grabbed my saxophone. For the rest of the night, we practiced until we had our song down perfectly.

"Guys!" I said, fist-bumping everyone. "That was awesome!"

Quentin smiled. "We're so going to win a trophy!"

"You know it, dude!" Kara added. "Morgan and the rest of Band 217 will eat our musical dust."

I hadn't even thought about that until now. What if one of the bands I was in won a trophy, and one didn't? I'd feel sort of bad.

"What's wrong, Colby?" Lexie asked.

"Nothing." I shrugged.

"I know," Quentin said. Then he talked in a baby voice. "Colby doesn't want his wittle girlfwiend's wittle feewings to be hurted when she's not awarded a shiny trophy."

It wasn't that. Morgan was seriously just a friend, no matter what Quentin said.

"Maybe it's weird, but I kind of feel like a cheater," I admitted then. "I mean, you guys know about Band 217, but Band 217 doesn't know about Four Ever."

"Don't worry about it," Kara said.

"Yeah." Quentin laughed. "Band 217 will find out soon enough at Amateur Night."

The day before Amateur Night, I made up my mind. Band 217 wouldn't find out tomorrow about our secret Four Ever band. Tonight, at our last practice, I'd tell them the truth. Right after Morgan took roll.

But I didn't get a chance because Morgan went right into, "Miles and Baylor have been working hard creating our band's website. Before we get started with practice tonight, I thought you'd all like to see it before it goes live, just in time for Amateur Night."

"Yeah!" Everyone cheered.

"Take it away, Miles!" Morgan said.

Miles wheeled himself up to the front of the garage, and everyone gathered around him and the laptop he'd brought. With just a few clicks, we were looking at a silvery background with music notes at the top. Each music note had a different letter and number on it to spell out BAND 217.

"That's cool, Miles!" I said.

"Thanks!" Miles said. "But wait until you see this." He clicked on the About Us page, and a picture of everyone in the band popped up. Miles took the pictures a few days ago. And below each picture was a bio Baylor had written.

"Hey, I'm a star!" Sherman said, pointing to his picture.

Hope laughed. "You mean I'm a star, right?"

"We're all stars!" I said. "But Miles and Baylor are superstars for creating this awesome website."

Davis started clapping then, and everyone joined in.

"Okay," Morgan said, holding up her hands. "Now it's time to get serious again and begin practicing."

This was my chance to tell everyone about my secret band with Quentin, Kara, and Lexie before I lost my nerve. "Before we get started," I began, "I need to talk to you guys."

Morgan frowned. "Colby, please. Our time is valuable, and we can't waste a minute of it on chitchat."

"But—," I tried again.

This time, Morgan did a big huffy breath. "Seriously, Colby! This time tomorrow night, we'll

be playing our very first gig. I doubt what you have to say is more important than that," she said. "So it can wait. Okay?"

I guessed Morgan was right. What I had to say would have to wait until tomorrow night. Hey, at least I tried.

So Morgan stood in front of us, clapped her hands, and said, "One and two and ready and play!"

For our song, we'd finally settled on "Love Me Tender," a classic by Elvis Presley. And Yulia's voice sounded tender and sweet as she sang the words to the King of Rock and Roll's hit.

Even though we sounded pretty awesome, Morgan insisted we play it again and again. The last time, she said, "Play like the musicians you are!"

"Hey!" Sherman said. "That's Mr. Byrd's line."

Morgan just smiled and counted us into the song again. When we finished the last line—"And I always will"—Morgan checked her watch. She said, "Okay, everyone, that's a wrap. And don't stay up late tonight. Everyone needs the extra z's."

"*Mademoiselle*," Lem said, "what should we wear?"

"I'm glad you asked that, Lem. Everyone should try to color coordinate. Let's stick with basic black and white and maybe gray. Those colors are classic, just like our song choice."

"Will this work?" I joked, pointing at my T-shirt. "It's white."

Morgan wrinkled her nose. "Look your best tomorrow, people! Remember, the Amateur Night audience will be huge, and they'll all be looking at us."

"A huge audience?" Yulia said then. "Do you really think there'll be that many people there?"

"Trust me, there'll be tons," Morgan said.

I wasn't so sure that was what Yulia hoped to hear because she didn't look so good then. She turned a funny shade of alien green just talking about tomorrow night. But she'd better get over it fast. In less than twenty-four hours, Band 217 would make its debut.

Chapter 10

MEET THE GEEKS

Morgan wasn't kidding. On Friday, Jazz Front's parking lot was packed with cars. And a stage had been set up in the lot behind the building for the Amateur Night performers.

All of the musicians had to sign in when they got there. So far, I'd met up with Band 217, but I hadn't seen anyone from Four Ever yet. I hoped they got here soon. Bands were set to perform in a certain order. And I'd seen that Four Ever played right after Band 217.

"Guys, I don't feel so great," Yulia said.

"You're fine," Morgan reassured her. "Trust me, a little bit of stage fright is normal."

"What about a lot of stage fright? Is that normal, too?" Yulia asked.

I fanned her with the program some guy handed me when we registered. "Better?" I asked.

Yulia only nodded.

"Colby!" Kara waved and made her way toward me, with Quentin and Lexie right behind her. "We finally made it!"

"Did you sign us in yet?" Quentin asked.

I made a slashing sign next to my throat, hoping Quentin would get the message and cut it out. I still hadn't had a chance to tell Morgan and the others about our secret band yet.

Quentin said, "Sorry, man. I thought they knew."

Morgan frowned. "What's he talking about, Colby?"

"Yeah, about that," I began. "See, it's a long story."

Morgan folded her arms across her chest. "That's cool. We've got plenty of time."

Now I knew what an interrogation felt like. I had no choice. It was time to come clean. And that's exactly what I did. I spilled my guts all over the place about the secret band that Kara, Quentin, Lexie, and I were in. I finished with, "Our band's name is Four Ever. And signing up our other band for Amateur Night was what Kara whispered to me the day she quit this band."

"You mean, you're actually in two bands?" Morgan said.

I nodded. "You've got it."

Sherman looked horrified. "What a tangled web you've weaved, Colby Ellis!"

"Yeah, he's been two-timing our band," Davis said.

"That's a twist," Baylor jumped in.

Morgan folded her arms. "It sure is."

"But why would you do this, Colby?" Miles asked.

I explained it all to them, just like I had to Rube last week. I told them about my dream of having my own band. But then Morgan pushed her way in as the bandleader. And the other kids pushed their way in, too. "At first, I didn't want to play with anyone from Room 217," I said.

"Why? Do you hate us so much that you didn't even want to hang out with us?" Baylor asked, like she was interviewing me for one of her school paper articles.

"No!" I shook my head. "It's not like that at all. It's just—"

"Go on," Hope said.

I swallowed hard. I'd just put everything out there. No more secrets. Not even my biggest secret. The one I didn't want the kids from our school band to know.

"The truth is, I'm not some great saxophone player," I began. "I'm nowhere near as good as the rest of you. I thought I could sort of hide it in our school band room because there are so many kids in there. But if you joined my garage band, I knew you'd all find out the truth."

Nobody said anything, so I took a deep breath and went on.

"Now that you know the truth, I just hope you don't all hate me. I didn't want you guys to find out like this. Honest." I smiled a little. "I tried to tell you about it yesterday at practice. But Morgan said it had to wait because there wasn't time for chitchat. You wouldn't listen."

"We're not listening now, either," Morgan said.

My smile faded. "I don't blame you."

"No, I don't mean we're not listening because we're mad at you," Morgan said. "Rube is motioning for us to come over to the stage."

She started to take off, and I called, "Wait! If you guys don't want me to perform with Band 217 tonight, I totally understand."

"Dude, now you're just being dumb," Davis said, smiling. "Of course you're playing with us. Duh!"

I looked at Morgan, waiting to see if she was going to tell me to get lost. But she smiled, too, when she said, "Duh! You're our band founder. We can't ax you. So let's go!"

We all followed Morgan over toward Rube.

"Boys and girls," Rube said, "you're our first band to perform tonight."

"F-f-first?" Yulia stuttered.

Rube nodded. "Get up there on that stage, and get ready while I welcome all of these fine people."

While we got our instruments set up, Rube thanked everyone for coming out to Jazz Front's First Annual Amateur Night.

"Ladies and gentleman, you're in for a treat," Rube said into the microphone. "Benton Bluff is home to some of the best musicians on the planet. And our first group to perform is no exception." He looked over at us. "Everyone, put your hands together for Band 217!"

People clapped like crazy. And Quentin gave me a thumbs-up from the front row, where he stood with Kara and Lexie.

On Morgan's count, we began playing "Love Me Tender." But Yulia never kicked in with the vocals. She just stood there behind the microphone stand. So Morgan signaled for us to stop the music.

Morgan went over and whispered something to Yulia. When Yulia nodded, Morgan went back to her place in front of the band and counted, "One and two and ready and go!"

For the second time, the band began playing. But Yulia's voice was still a no-show. Morgan cut the music again.

This was not good. I looked out into the audience. People stared at us, waiting for something. Anything. Then I got an idea. Real quick, I ran it by Morgan. When she agreed, I motioned for Quentin and Kara to bring their instruments up onstage. Lexie came up, too.

"Change of plans," I whispered. "We're going to play 'The Star Spangled Banner.' It's something everyone knows."

Lem freaked out. "But we don't have any sheet music, *monsieur*."

"It's okay," I said. "We've played it a hundred times in the band room." I pointed to my head. "We've all got it right here. Just trust yourselves."

On Morgan's count, we all began playing. Lexie didn't miss a beat. "O! Say can you see, by the dawn's early light," she belted out.

Halfway through the song, Yulia found her voice, too. She and Lexie finished the song

together. And on that last note, the entire crowd was on their feet.

"Whoo-wee!" Rube said as the crowd cheered. "What a way to kick off Amateur Night! Let's hear it one more time for Band 217!"

After everyone cleared the stage, Rube announced, "Our national anthem has rarely sounded better. To keep the patriotic theme going, please welcome Four Ever as they play the beautiful 'My Country, 'Tis of Thee.'"

So for the second time, Kara, Quentin, Lexie, and I went back up onstage. And our performance went just like we'd rehearsed. Perfect!

When we came off the stage, everyone from Band 217 was there to meet us.

"You guys killed it!" Davis said.

Baylor nodded. "You were totally ah-mazing!"

"Everyone, I'm really sorry," Yulia said then. "I let you down up there tonight. I just choked."

"It's cool," Sherman said. "Stuff like that happens sometimes. And she saved the day." He pointed at Lexie.

"She did save us," Morgan agreed. "But that was all this guy's idea." And she pointed at me.

I smiled. "Hey, that's what friends do."

"Yeah, about that," Morgan said. "I'm afraid I haven't been too friendly. I'm just so into music that I didn't realize how pushy I was. I'm sorry, Colby." Then she looked at Kara and Quentin. "And I'm sorry I was so bossy. Sheet music is good and all.

But sometimes, you have to know it here, too." She pointed at her head, just like I did earlier.

"Right on!" Kara said. "Apology accepted."

Morgan smiled. "Maybe you guys would consider rejoining our band. And you, too," she said to Lexie.

"Yeah," I said. "We'll merge our bands together, sort of like the merge on that TV show."

"*Survivor*!" Miles added. "And there's room for three more band members on our website."

"Not so fast," Quentin said. "We're not all in your school band, so I'm not joining unless we change the band name."

"To what?" Baylor asked.

Nobody had any ideas.

"I can't believe it!" I joked. "All of us Band Geeks, and nobody can think of a band name."

Everyone laughed.

But then I said, "Hey, that's it! What if we call ourselves the Band Geeks?"

"I like it!" Quentin said.

Morgan and everyone else agreed to our new name, too.

So we hung out listening to the other bands after that. And when it was time for the awards ceremony, Rube announced, "Second place goes to Band 217, accompanied by Four Ever!"

After we accepted our trophy, Rube whispered, "What band have you decided to stay in, Colby?"

"Both!" I said.

Rube looked surprised.

"We worked everything out," I explained. "Band isn't about the skills, Rube. It's all about the people, you know."

"I think I've heard that before." Rube laughed.

I laughed, too. Then I introduced Rube to my new, old band—the Band Geeks.